Who's Awake in Springtime?

Phillis Gershator and Mim Green
illustrated by Emilie Chollat

Christy Ottaviano Books
Henry Holt and Company ❋ New York

Henry Holt and Company, LLC
Publishers since 1866
175 Fifth Avenue
New York, New York 10010
www.HenryHoltKids.com

Library of Congress Cataloging-in-Publication Data
Gershator, Phillis.
Who's awake in springtime? / by Phillis Gershator and Mim Green ;
illustrated by Emilie Chollat. — 1st ed.
p.   cm.
"Christy Ottaviano Books."
Summary: Describes, in rhymed cumulative text and
illustrations, how various young animals and one small
human prepare for sleep at the end of the day.
ISBN 978-0-8050-6390-5
[1. Stories in rhyme. 2. Bedtime—Fiction. 3. Animals—
Infancy—Fiction.] I. Green, Mim. II. Chollat, Emilie, ill.
III. Title. IV. Title: Who is awake in springtime.
PZ8.3.G3235Who 2010   [E]—dc22   2009009224

First Edition—2010 / Designed by Véronique Lefèvre Sweet
Printed in October 2009 in China by South China Printing
Company Ltd., Dongguan City, Guangdong Province,
on acid-free paper. ∞
The artist used acrylics and collage on Lavis paper
to create the illustrations for this book.

10 9 8 7 6 5 4 3 2 1

To Natalie, Zori, Edna, and Christy
—P. G. and M. G.

For Madeleine, my sassy little one
—E. C.

Down, down goes the sun,
And down in the sea,
Fish find a safe place to hide.

Who's asleep?

"Not I," says the minnow.

In a pond by the sea,
Ducks tuck their heads
Under their wings.

Who's asleep?

"Not I," says the duckling.

In the tall green grass
Near the pond by the sea,
Turtles pull their heads and tails
Into their shells.

Who's asleep?

"Not I," says the little turtle.

In a garden near the grass
Near the pond by the sea,
Bees buzz home.

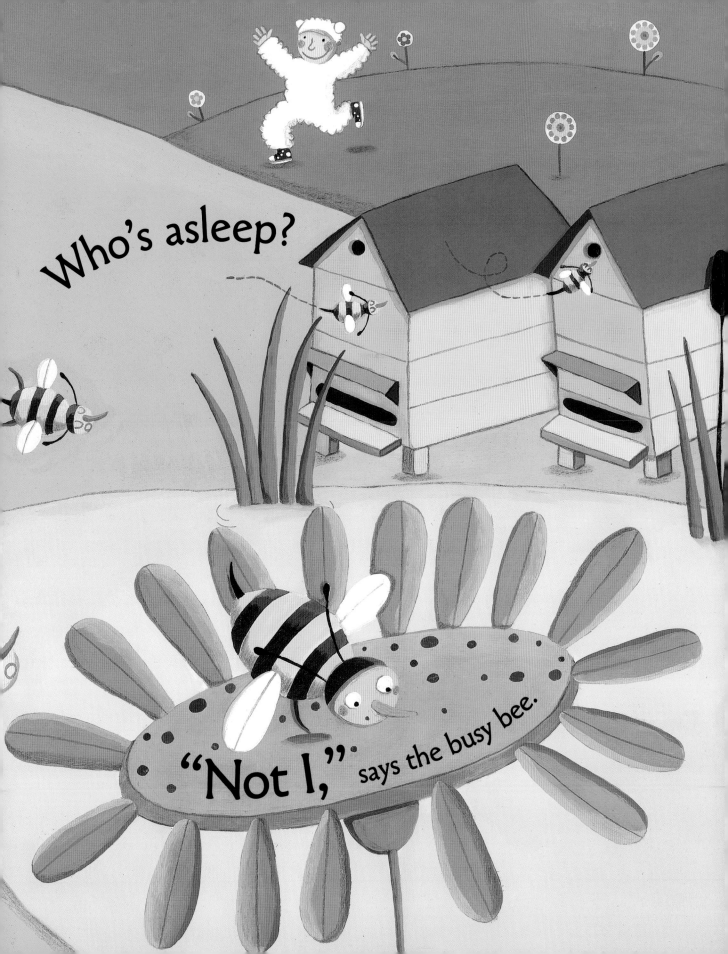

In the branches of a leafy tree
Near the garden
Near the grass
Near the pond by the sea,
Birds nestle in their nests.

Who's asleep?

In a patch of clover
Near the leafy tree
Near the garden
Near the grass
Near the pond by the sea,
Cats curl up and close their eyes.

Who's
asleep?

"Not I," says the kitten.

In a bush
  Near the clover
   Near the leafy tree
    Near the garden
     Near the grass
      Near the pond by the sea,
       Caterpillars spin their silken beds.

Who's asleep?

"Not I," says the small green caterpillar.

Over in the meadow
Where wildflowers grow,
Up, up comes the moon,
And down below,
Near the bush near the clover
Near the leafy tree
Near the garden near the grass
Near the pond by the sea,
Sheep huddle and cuddle in their
warm wool coats.

Who's asleep?

"Not I,"
says the lamb.

"Not I. Not I.
We like to play!"

Sheep follow sheep,
Jumping high, jumping low.
Sheep follow sheep.
Now where did they go?

To sleep, to sleep.
The sheep went to sleep!

Not the sheep.
Not the caterpillars.
Not the cats.
Not the birds in the leafy tree.
Not the bees.
Not the turtles.
Not the ducks.
Not the fish down in the sea.

Is anyone awake?

Then come jump into bed,
My sweet little lamb.